For Joni from Zeyde Mick
MR

For all the children and staff at Albert Pye Nursery
PD

First US edition 2022 • First published by Walker Books Ltd. (UK) 2022

Library of Congress Catalog Card Number pending • ISBN 978-1-5362-2497-9

22 23 24 25 26 27 APS 10 9 8 7 6 5 4 3 2 1

Printed in Humen, Dongguan, China

This book was typeset in Avenir. • The illustrations were done in ink and watercolor and finished digitally.

Candlewick Press • 99 Dover Street • Somerville, Massachusetts 02144 • www.candlewick.com

Ready for Spaghetti

Funny Poems for Funny Kids

Michael Rosen   illustrated by **Polly Dunbar**

CANDLEWICK PRESS

A Note to Grown-Ups

By the time we're about three years old, we have learned all the sounds of our language. How do we do it? Mostly through a mix of copying the words of the people around us and inventing sounds of our own. At the same time, our brains are discovering how things work: how, if you drop a spoon, it lands on the floor and stays there; how food can be hot or cold, sticky or smooth; how a ball rolls and water flows; how blocks can be piled up or knocked down . . . and hundreds of other things that we take for granted when we're just a few years older.

To figure these things out, we need to explore how words and language mean stuff—and how they're not just a stream of sounds. Books can play a fantastic part in all this: they help children to link words with grammar and pictures, and learn how language fits together when it's written down (which is very different from the way people chat to each other out loud). Introducing children to the sound of writing is a great way for them to get the hang of its meaning.

One way to make this fun is with rhyme, rhythm, repetition, and play. That's where I come in! I've written the poems in this book so that a child will be tickled by the sounds they like, and what they mean, on a journey through their day—from sunup to lights-out. I hope that they will copy the sounds and play with words, and that this helps them to discover that talking is about choosing what we want to say . . . one of the most powerful bits of knowledge there is.

If you're reading this book out loud, feel free to repeat things, or change things, or turn the poems into chants or songs, or tap out the rhythms with your fingers, a spoon, or anything else. There's all sorts to explore in Polly Dunbar's wonderful pictures, too, so there are plenty of things to talk about. And if your child makes up rhymes or plays with words, why not write these down and read them back? Why not get some colors out and do some pictures together, too?

Above all else, I hope you enjoy the trip!

Michael Rosen

Up!

Up, up, uppity-up!

The light shines through the window

Up, up, uppity-up!

Here is my nose and here's my elbow

Up, up, uppity-up!

My feet are standing on the floor

Up, up, uppity-up!

My feet are taking me out the door

Mirror

There's someone in the mirror.

Look, can you see?

It looks like they're talking.

Is it them? Is it me?

I've gone away now—

I'm not saying where.

I can't see the mirror.

Am I still there?

Where's My Brush?

I'm all in a rush.
Where's my brush?
I've got to brush my teeth!

Rushy, rushy, rushy
Brushy, brushy, brushy
Bsssh! Bsssh! Bsssh!

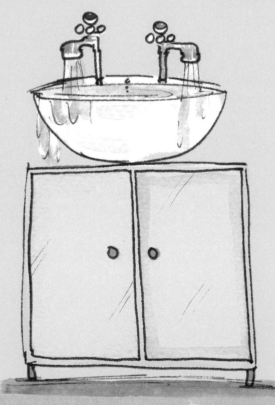

I'm all in a hurry—
I'm all in a worry.
I've got to have a wash!

Hurry, hurry, hurry
Worry, worry, worry
Whoosh! Whoosh! Whoosh!

I really hope
I can find the soap . . .
A-splish, a-splash, a-splosh!

Washy, washy, washy
Sploshy, sploshy, sploshy
Sploosh! Sploosh! Sploosh!

Tummy Rumbles

Mummy, mommy,

mumbly mumbles.

Grummy, grommy,

grumbly grumbles.

Bammy, bimmy,

bumbly bumbles.

Jammy, jimmy,

jumbly jumbles.

Timmy, tummy,

tumbly tumbles . . .

Now my tummy

rumbly rumbles.

Long Leggy Eggy

Long leggy eggy . . .

has a hard shell.

Long leggy eggy . . .

well, well, well.

Long leggy eggy . . .

sitting in your cup.

Long leggy eggy . . .

gobble you up!

Here They Come

Here come my floppy shoes

flip flap flappety flap

Here come my clippy shoes

trip trap trappety trap

Here come my clappy hands

clip clap clappety clap

Here come my slappy hands

slip slap slappety slap

Here comes an egg for me

tip tap tappety tap

Here comes some sleep for me

nip nap nappety nap

Hip **Hap Happy**

Give me a **hip**

Give me a **hap**

Give me a hip **hap happy**

Give me a **tip**

Give me a **tap**

Give me a tip **tap tappy**

Give me a **pip**

Give me a **pap**

Give me a pip **pap pappy**

Give me a **zip**

Give me a **zap**

Give me a zip **zap zappy**

11

Silly Old Sun

Silly old sun,
doing the same old thing
day after day after day.

Silly old sun,
coming up after dark
in the same old silly way.

Silly old sun,
you should do something new
like coming out in the night.

If you did
it would change a lot—
you'd make the night sky bright.

Come Back Soon

I had a balloon
That was all my own.
I loved my balloon—
I tied it to a stone.

I told the balloon
To stay right there.
I told the balloon:
"Don't go anywhere!"

I went to get dressed—
I put my clothes on—
But when I got back
My balloon had gone.

Oh, balloon! Oh, balloon!
Please come back soon!
Please come back . . .
Oh, balloon. Oh, balloon.

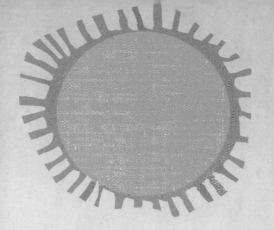

Hello, You

Hello, you! Hello!
Hello, them! Hello, me!
Hello yellow yellow!

Hi to you! Hi!
Hi to them and me!
Hi-tee-tooty-tie!

16

Hello, Cloud

Hello, cloud in the sky!

I'm going to put you in a cup,

stir you round and round,

and drink you all up.

Raining Flowers

One day it rained flowers
for hours and hours.
For hours and hours
it was raining flowers.

One day it rained peas
all over our knees.
All over our knees
it was raining peas.

One day it rained rain
again and again.
Again and again
it was raining rain.

Bumblebee
and Butterfly

Bumblebee rumble,

Bumblebee tumble,

Buzzy bee bumble . . .

Give me apple crumble!

Butterfly fly,

Butterfly high,

Flitter flutter by . . .

Give me apple pie!

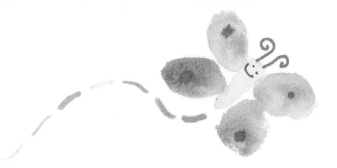

Snail

Snail, Snail,
will you tell me a tale?
Tell me a tale
as long as your trail!

Snail, Snail,
what tale will you tell?
Will you tell me a tale
of you in your shell?

Paddling Pool

Phew!

I'm so hot.

I'm so, so hot.

I've jumped in the paddling pool

and now I'm not.

Whoosh!

I'm so wet.

I'm so, so wet.

Jump out of the

paddling pool . . .

Now **EVERYBODY'S** wet!

Sandbox

Here's my castle.

Don't you think it's grand?

But—oops!—it falls over

'cause it's made of sand.

Digger

Big, big digger . . .

Bigger and bigger!

Dig, dig, digger!

Big dig, digger!

Digger-doo, digger—

Bigger-boo, bigger!

Diggy-dig, digger—

Biggy-big, bigger!

On the Swings

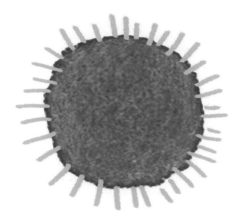

Swing me on the swing,
Higher and higher and higher.
I'm a swingy flyer!
Higher and higher and higher.

Swing me on the swing,
Push me, push me, push.
I go swooshy-swoosh!
Push me, push me, push.

Swing me on the swing,

Swinging and swinging and swinging.

Swing me on the swing,

I'm singing and singing and singing.

Ready for Spaghetti

I'm ready for spaghetti.

Will you getti the spaghetti?

Don't say, "Not yetti spaghetti!"

I'm all setti for spaghetti.

Make a Cake

Today
is birthday-day.
Birthday-day
all day.

Make a cake,
bake a cake,
put the candles on top.

Time to eat,

what a treat.

Never, never stop!

31

Give Me an ABC

Hey, come on!
Let's do this:

Give me an **A** then a **B**
Give me a **C** then a **D**
Clap your hands
And it's **E F G**

Then it's **H I J**
Give me a **K**
Then it's **L** and **M**
Give me an **N**

32

Now it's **O P Q**
And **R S T**
Then follow that
With a **U** and a **V**

I know who
It's a **W**

X Y Z,

sleep for me.

Grover Fell Over

This is my friend Grover.

Yesterday, he fell over.

Grover fell over and over!

When Grover fell over,
he shouted out: *"Ow!"*
After that shout,
he said, "I'm OK now."

This is my friend Grover.
Yesterday, he fell over.
Grover fell over and over . . .

but he's OK now.

Teddy

Teddy knows
he's got a nose,
I suppose.

Teddy thinks
he can wink,
I think.

"Will Teddy play
today?"
I say.

Will Teddy say yes?
Yes,
I guess!

Jumping!

Jump up, jump up,

We're jumping, jumping,

Can you see us jump?

Jump up, jump up,

We're jumping, jumping,

And landing with a bump.

Throw a Ball

Show a ball
Throw a ball
Bouncy, bouncy, bouncy!

Roll a ball
Bowl a ball
Bouncy, bouncy, bouncy . . .

Drop a ball
Stop a ball
Bouncy . . . bouncy . . . b o u n c y . . . STOP!

39

The Itch

"Hello," said the itch,
"I've been looking for you.
   I'm ready to sit on your arm."

"I'm not bad," said the itch,
"I won't be here long,
   I won't do you any harm."

The itch jumped up,
   did a hop and a skip—
   it was much too hard to catch.

It did just as it said:
   it landed on my arm . . .
   and then I started to scratch.

The Sneeze

Help!

Oh, please!

I'm going to sneeze.

I think it all started

When I ate a bit of cheese.

One . . .

Two . . .

Let's count to ten.

Atishoo! Atishoo!

Atishoo once again!

Where's the sneeze gone?

I'm going to guess:

It started in my nose

And ended in a mess.

Water Over My Toes

Water washes
over my toes,
splishes and sploshes—
see how it goes?

Bubbles are bubbly,
Ripples are ripply,
Waves are wavy . . .
Trickles are trickly!

Water washes
over my toes,
splishes and sploshes—
see how it goes?

Bubble

Bibble, bobble, bubble,

Dibble, dobble, double . . .

You can't catch the bubble,

The bubble can't catch me.

Stipple, stopple, stop,

Pipple, popple, pop . . .

I *did* catch the bubble—

Now there's no bubble to see!

Jimmy Jams

Jimmy jammy 'jamas
in my bed.
Jimmy jammy 'jamas
on my head.

Jimmy jammy 'jamas

flying through the air.

Jimmy jammy 'jamas

on Teddy Bear!

The Stars

I stare at the stars—
the stars stare at me.
Are you listening?
Can you see what I see?

I wave to the stars—
the stars wave at me.
Are you listening?
Can you see what I see?

48

I sing to the stars—
the stars sing to me.
Are you listening?
Can you see what I see?

Good night to the stars
and good night to me.
Are you listening?
Can you see what I see?

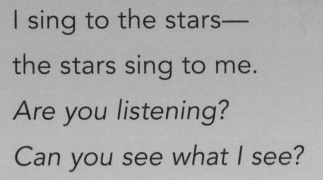

Good Night!

Hush and a hush
Come what may
Hush and a hush
At the end of the day

Hush and a hush
Makes it just so
Hush and a hush
Soft and low

50

Hush and a hush
Through the air
Hush and a hush
Here and there

Hush and a hush
Do what's right
Hush and a hush
Say "Good night!"

Index